D1529715

Spaghetti Smiles

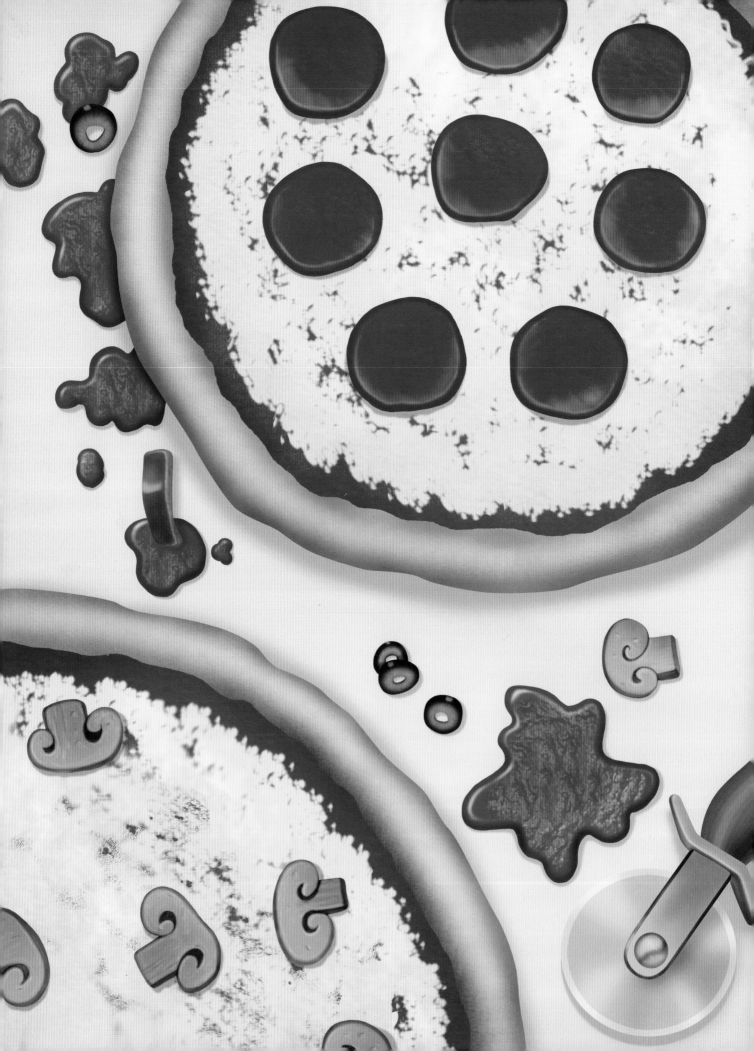

Spaghetti Smiles

By Margo Sorenson
Illustrated by David Harrington

PELICAN PUBLISHING COMPANY

GRETNA 2014

For the Adorables, with love and aloha: Carson Williams, Maren Jill, Samantha Kate, and Taylor Jane

—M.S.

To my wonderful neices Elise and Sabrina

—D.H.

The word "Pelican" and the depiction of a pelican are trademarks of Pelican Publishing Company, Inc., and are registered in the U.S. Patent and Trademark Office.

Library of Congress Cataloging-in-Publication Data

Sorenson, Margo.
  Spaghetti smiles / by Margo Sorenson ; illustrated by David Harrington.
     pages cm
  Summary: Rocco's Italian Restaurant needs a new neighbor and Rocco's nephew, Jake, sets out to find one but while everyone in town loves the food, they do not want to move next to such a crazy, mixed-up restaurant.
  ISBN 978-1-4556-1922-1 (hardcover : alk. paper) -- ISBN 978-1-4556-1923-8 (e-book) [1. Restaurants--Fiction. 2. City and town life--Fiction. 3. Books and reading--Fiction. 4. Humorous stories.] I. Harrington, David, illustrator. II. Title.
  PZ7.S72147Sp 2014
  [E]--dc23
                          2013046433

Printed in Malaysia

Published by Pelican Publishing Company, Inc.
1000 Burmaster Street, Gretna, Louisiana 70053

SPAGHETTI SMILES

Jake rushed into Rocco's Italian Restaurant.
"Uncle Rocco!" Jake said, "I have a new book
to read to you!"

"*Ciao*, Jake," Uncle Rocco sighed. "I don't think you'll be able to read to me in the restaurant anymore. I have big problems!"
"What happened?" Jake asked.

"My restaurant needs a new neighbor. We need someone who likes to have fun," Uncle Rocco said.

"What happens if you don't find one?"
Jake asked.

"I would have to close my restaurant,"
Uncle Rocco replied. "No more reading
time for us."

Uncle Rocco tried to make happy faces on the pizzas.

But the pepperoni smiles wilted.

Jake exclaimed, "I'll find you a neighbor!"

"But everybody knows this is a crazy, mixed-up restaurant," Uncle Rocco said.

"Everyone likes to eat here and have fun,"
Jake said. "Remember how we play spaghetti
pick-up sticks?"
"And bowl with mozzarella balls, knocking
over olive oil," Uncle Rocco added.

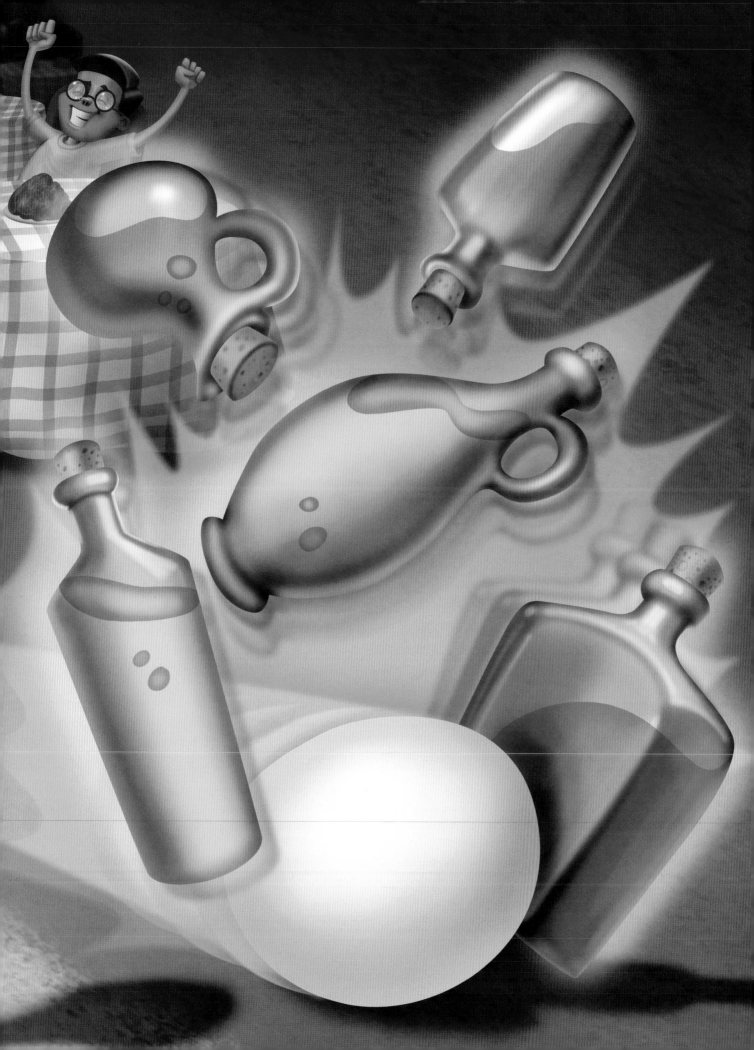

"Who wouldn't want to be next door?" Uncle Rocco asked, juggling ravioli.

First, Jake went to see Ms. Cash at the bank. She was working at the front desk.

"Ms. Cash," Jake said. "Would you like to move the bank next door to Rocco's Italian Restaurant?"

"I don't think so, Jake," she said.

"Why not?" he asked.

"Bank customers would get pepperoni slices instead of quarters. I'd find rows of pizzas baking in the bank vault."

Jake sighed.

"But tell Rocco," Ms. Cash said, "it's the best Italian food in town!"

Jake thanked Mrs. Cash and left the bank. She definitely needed some pizzas baking in her bank vault.

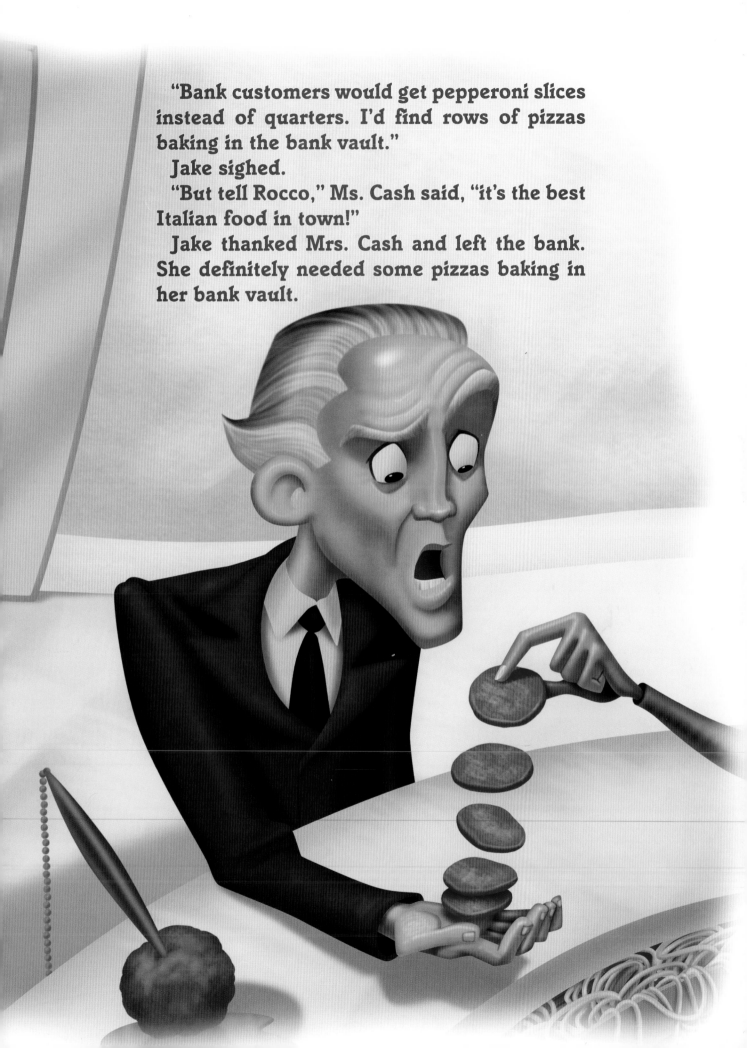

Jake opened the post office door. Mr. Stamply was stamping envelopes.

"Mr. Stamply," Jake called. "Why don't you move the post office next door to Rocco's Italian Restaurant?"

"Move next door to Rocco? I don't think so," said Mr. Stamply.

"Why not?" Jake asked.

Mr. Stamply said, "Pepperoncini on envelopes instead of stamps? Lasagna would be airmailed all over the world!" He grinned at Jake. "But tell Rocco I'll be there for dinner."

Jake thanked Mr. Stamply. He'd ask Rocco to mail him some lasagna just for fun.

Jake walked to Mr. Pumper's gas station.
Mr. Pumper was tinkering with a car.
"Hi," Jake said. "Wouldn't you like to move
in next door to Rocco's Italian Restaurant?"

"My gas station?" Mr. Pumper asked. "The gas pumps would pump tomato sauce instead of gas. Customers would get olive oil added to their engines instead of motor oil!" He looked at Jake. "Nope. But tell Rocco his spaghetti is still the greatest!"

Jake sighed. Just think how smoothly an engine would run after it got its olive oil!

Jake walked farther and farther. His head sank lower and lower.

Finally, he stood at the very edge of town and looked back down Main Street. He could see Uncle Rocco's restaurant. The bright red and green and white sign looked cheerful, but Jake didn't feel cheerful at all.

He sat down on a bench to think. As he looked up, he read the sign on the new store in front of him.

Bright red and green letters spelled out "Page's Bookstore."

Maybe a bookstore would work!

"A customer! A customer!" a roly-poly lady exclaimed. "I'm Mrs. Page! Welcome to my new bookstore! I didn't think anyone in this town read books. No one comes here," she said. "Doesn't anyone like to have fun?" she asked.

"I'm Jake," Jake said. "My uncle owns Rocco's Italian Restaurant. I . . . I didn't come here to buy a book," he admitted.

Mrs. Page's face lost its smile. "You didn't come to buy a book?" she asked.

"But, wait," Jake said. "I'm looking for a new neighbor for my Uncle Rocco's restaurant in the middle of town."

"In the middle of town . . ." Mrs. Page repeated slowly. She looked thoughtful for a moment.

"Everyone would buy your books and
then eat next door," Jake said. "Or they
could eat at Rocco's first. Then, they
could buy a book from you for dessert!"

"But what if people use pasta for bookmarks," Mrs. Page asked, "or find anchovies on the shelves?"

Jake said, "If people are having fun reading books, what does it matter?"

"Oh!" she exclaimed. "Wonderful! And I'll help you find books to read."

"It's a deal," he said. "Thanks!"

He hurried back to Uncle Rocco's.

"Uncle Rocco!" he called. "I found the perfect neighbor for your restaurant—Mrs. Page and her new bookstore! Everyone in town will line up to eat at your restaurant. Then they can buy a book next door. Mrs. Page promised to help me find good books to read to you, too!"

"I can't wait to hear you read!" Rocco said, grinning. "Come!"
    Jake followed Rocco into the kitchen.
    And together, they turned all the pepperoni mouths on the pizzas into curvy smiles!